The Berenstain Bears
and the
DOUBLE DARE

When peer pressure rears its ugly head, it's easy for most cubs to be misled.

A FIRST TIME BOOK®

The Berenstain Bears

and the

DOUBLE

Stan & Jan Berenstain

Random House New York

DARE

Library of Congress Cataloging-in-Publication Data: Berenstain, Stan. The Berenstain Bears and the double dare / Stan & Jan Berenstain.   p. cm.—(A First time book)   SUMMARY: Brother Bear feels excited about joining Too-Tall Grizzly's gang until the members dare him to steal one of Farmer Ben's juicy watermelons. ISBN: 0-394-89748-X (pbk); 0-394-99748-4 (lib. bdg.)   [1. Conduct of life—Fiction.   2. Bears—Fiction.] I. Berenstain, Jan.   II. Title.   III. Series: Berenstain, Stan.   First time books.   PZ7.B4483Bejk 1988   [E]—dc19   87-27296

Manufactured in the United States of America   22   23   24   25   26   27   28   29   30

It was one of those days in Bear Country when everything was going so well, you just knew that any minute something was bound to go wrong.

Papa Bear was off chopping wood in the forest, Mama Bear was putting in some tomato plants, Brother Bear was working on a tangled fishing line...

...and Sister Bear was running
up the front path as upset as
she could be.

"Mama! Mama!" she shouted.

"What is it, sweetie?" asked Mama.

"They took—they took—" Sister was so angry she could hardly speak.

"Calm down, dear," said Mama, "and tell us what happened."

"Some big cubs at the playground took my jump rope and won't give it back," Sister said.

Mama wanted to hear more, but Brother had heard quite enough. He just knew it was those troublemakers Too-Tall Grizzly and his gang, bothering smaller cubs again. So off he stalked, heading straight for the playground.

Not only were Too-Tall and his gang still there, but Too-Tall was jumping with Sister's rope.

"Onesie, twosie, I love yousie," he sang in a mocking tone. "Threesie, foursie, shut the doorsie."

"That's my sister's rope!" shouted Brother.
"Give it back, you big oaf!"

"Or what?" sneered Too-Tall.

"Or I may have to cut you down to
size," said Brother, reaching for
the rope.

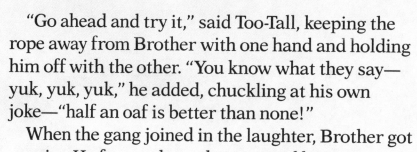

"Go ahead and try it," said Too-Tall, keeping the rope away from Brother with one hand and holding him off with the other. "You know what they say— yuk, yuk, yuk," he added, chuckling at his own joke—"half an oaf is better than none!"

When the gang joined in the laughter, Brother got angrier. He forgot about the rope and began swinging wildly at Too-Tall.

"Why don't you stop bothering my sister," Brother said, "and pick on somebody your own size?"

"Why don't *you* pick on somebody *your* own size?" said Too-Tall, grinning. "And anyway, here's your sister's dopey rope back."

"Huh?" said Brother, more than a little confused. "Well, uh—thanks, I guess. I'll be going now. See you."

"Hey! Wait a minute!" called Too-Tall. "I might be able to use a cub like you. You've got moxie."

"Moxie?" said Brother.

"Yeah. Spunk. Nerve. Moxie." He put a big arm around Brother's shoulders. "Why don't you come with us and have a little fun?"

The rest of the gang gathered around and Brother said, "I really think I better be go—"

"Whatsa matter?" said one. "Chicken?"

Another one began strutting, flapping his arms like a chicken, and clucking "Puk, puk, puk—*aaw!* Puk, puk, puk—*aaw!*" Pretty soon the whole gang was strutting and clucking all over the place.

"I am not chicken!" protested Brother.
"Prove it," said Too-Tall. "Come along
with us for some fun."

Brother was a little nervous about joining
the gang, but he certainly didn't want them
to think he was chicken. So when they
scampered off into the woods, he followed.

He got more and more nervous
as they led him along the
dangerous old quarry path,

across Roaring Creek,

and past the Spooky Old Tree.

After a few more twists and turns, Too-Tall signaled a stop. When Brother saw where they were, he was surprised and pleased.

"Hey!" he said. "This is Farmer Ben's watermelon pa—"

"Shhh!" hissed Too-Tall, clapping a hand over his mouth. "You want to spoil our fun?"

NO TRESPASSING
PRIVATE PROPERTY

It turned out that Too-Tall's idea of fun was to run off with one of Farmer Ben's watermelons. And as the newest member of the gang, Brother was the one who was expected to do it.

"But Farmer Ben is a friend of mine," he protested. "And besides, it isn't honest!"

The gang flapped their arms like chickens and clucked "Puk, puk, puk—*aaw!*" into Brother's ear.

"I'm not chicken!" Brother insisted.

"Then go ahead and take the watermelon," said Too-Tall. "Farmer Ben'll never miss it!"

Brother Bear looked all around. Ben
was nowhere to be seen and it *was* sort
of exciting being in the gang.

The dee-double dare did it. Ever
so quietly, ever so carefully, Brother
Bear crept through the tall grass,
through the fence, and past the NO
TRESPASSING, PRIVATE PROPERTY sign
and picked out the biggest, fattest,
greenest watermelon in the patch.
Then he broke off the stem, picked
it up, and—

"Gotcha! You thievin' varmit!" shouted a voice. Too-Tall and his gang ran away, leaving Brother Bear holding the watermelon. Farmer Ben had been hiding in the cornfield. When he saw who it was he had by the collar, he was almost as surprised as Brother.

"Brother Bear, what in the world are you doin' with that watermelon-stealin' Too-Tall?"

At first, Brother was so ashamed he couldn't answer. But then the whole story came tumbling out: how he got Sister's rope back, how they called him chicken, and how they dee-double-dared him.

"Well," said Ben as they walked through his chicken yard, "chickens aren't very bright. But they're too smart to do something stupid just because somebody calls them chicken."

"I guess so," admitted Brother.

Just ahead was the meadow where Ben's
sheep were grazing. One of them—a large
ram—took it into his head to start running.
And run he did—straight for the highway!

"Your sheep are headed for the highway, Ben!"
cried Brother.

"Don't worry," said Ben. "Shep, my old
sheepdog, will take care of 'em." Shep raced
ahead and cut the sheep off before they got there.

"Sheep are like that," said Ben. "Follow a leader anywhere—off a cliff, if that's what the leader decides. And some folks are like that too. Follow a leader wherever he goes—across a highway, over a cliff...to the edge of my watermelon patch." He looked at Brother, and Brother knew exactly what he was talking about.

"And speaking of watermelon— how about having a nice sweet juicy slice with me?"
"Could we?" asked Brother.

"Sure," said Ben, cutting a big center slice in half. "And remember—mmm, this is a good one—being part of a group is okay—and maybe even having a leader. But you always have to think for yourself—especially about important things like what's right and what's wrong, and what's safe and what's dangerous."

"I'll remember, Ben," said Brother. "And thanks for the watermelon."

Brother decided to head home by way of the highway. And who was waiting around the bend? The Too-Tall gang!

"What happened?" asked Too-Tall.

"Nothing much," answered Brother. "We had a little talk and some watermelon."

"Hey, cool," said Too-Tall. "Well, come on. We're goin' over to the Widder Bruin's and have a little *more* fun."

"*No possible way,*" said Brother.

"Whatsa matter?" sneered Too-Tall. "Chicken?"

"Puk, puk, puk—*aaw!*" clucked the gang.

"Baa! Baa! Buncha sheep!" answered Brother. "Why don't you try thinking for yourselves for a change?"

"Puk, puk, puk—*aaw!*" they shouted.

"Baa! Baa! Buncha sheep!" Brother shouted back.

But the cubs' shouting was interrupted by another noise: the sound of somebody crashing out of the woods.

He looked a lot like Too-Tall but was much, *much* bigger. It was Too-Tall's papa, Two-Ton Grizzly.

"Wh-wh-what's up, Pop?" asked Too-Tall.

"What's up," growled Two-Ton, "is a little phone call I had from Farmer Ben about you!

"And," he added as he turned to the gang,
"if I hear about any more shenanigans,
all your parents are gonna hear from *me*!
Now get on home!"

The gang got on home as fast
as their legs could carry them.

"Hi," said Brother to Sister when he got back to the tree house. "Here's your jump rope."

"Oh, thank you!" she said. "How did you ever get it back from that awful Too-Tall and his gang?"

Brother shrugged. "I asked them for it and they gave it back."

"Hmm," said Mama. "You asked them for it and they gave it back—just like that?"

"Well," said Brother, going back to his tangled fishing line, "not *exactly* just like that."

E   Berenstain, Stan.
BER   The Berenstain
            Bears and the
            double dare

PERMA-BOUND®

DATE DUE	Name		Room
3-10-02	Jengure	Pernadez	T16
4-14-04	Tuyet	Phung	42